BY ALLAN MOREY

THE KANSAS CITY CHIEFS STORY

TORQUE

BELLWETHER MEDIA · MINNEAPOLIS, MN

™

Are you ready to take it to the extreme? Torque books thrust you into the action-packed world of sports, vehicles, mystery, and adventure. These books may include dirt, smoke, fire, and chilling tales. **WARNING**: read at your own risk.

This edition first published in 2017 by Bellwether Media, Inc.

No part of this publication may be reproduced in whole or in part without written permission of the publisher. For information regarding permission, write to Bellwether Media, Inc., Attention: Permissions Department, 5357 Penn Avenue South, Minneapolis, MN 55419.

Library of Congress Cataloging-in-Publication Data

Names: Morey, Allan, author.
Title: The Kansas City Chiefs Story / by Allan Morey.
Description: Minneapolis, MN : Bellwether Media, Inc., 2017. | Series: Torque: NFL Teams | Includes index.
Identifiers: LCCN 2015049956 | ISBN 9781626173705 (hardcover : alk. paper)
Subjects: LCSH: Kansas City Chiefs (Football team)–History–Juvenile literature.
Classification: LCC GV956.K35 M67 2017 | DDC 796.332/6409778411–dc23
LC record available at http://lccn.loc.gov/2015049956

Printed in the United States of America, North Mankato, MN.

TABLE OF CONTENTS

It is the last game of the 2015 season. The Kansas City Chiefs face the Oakland Raiders. The Chiefs score first.

Jeremy Maclin

Spencer Ware

Quarterback Alex Smith slings the ball to **wide receiver** Jeremy Maclin. Touchdown! A little later, **running back** Spencer Ware busts into the end zone. Another touchdown!

5

D.J. Alexander

The Raiders come back with a field goal and a touchdown. The Chiefs are ahead by only 4 points at the half.

Early in the second half, the Chiefs' **defense** scores a safety. Minutes later, Smith tosses to **tight end** Demetrius Harris. Touchdown! The Chiefs go on to win 23 to 17. They are headed to the **playoffs**!

Demetrius Harris

SCORING TERMS

END ZONE
the area at each end of a football field; a team scores by entering the opponent's end zone with the football.

EXTRA POINT
a score that occurs when a kicker kicks the ball between the opponent's goal posts after a touchdown is scored; 1 point.

FIELD GOAL
a score that occurs when a kicker kicks the ball between the opponent's goal posts; 3 points.

SAFETY
a score that occurs when a player on offense is tackled behind his own goal line; 2 points for defense.

TOUCHDOWN
a score that occurs when a team crosses into its opponent's end zone with the football; 6 points.

TWO-POINT CONVERSION
a score that occurs when a team crosses into its opponent's end zone with the football after scoring a touchdown; 2 points.

The Kansas City Chiefs started strong as a **professional** football team. In their first ten seasons, they won three American Football League (AFL) titles and **Super Bowl** 4!

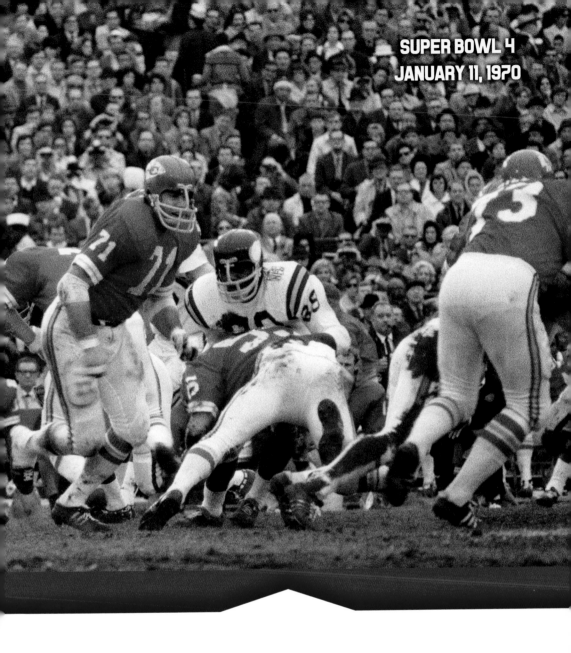

Their "smashmouth" style of **offense**
was key to their success. They had powerful
running backs moving the ball down the field.

ARROWHEAD STADIUM

Kansas City, Missouri, lies along the Missouri River. It is on the state's western border with Kansas. Fans in both states support the Chiefs.

The Chiefs have played home games at Arrowhead Stadium since 1972. Baseball's Kansas City Royals play in nearby Kauffman Stadium. Both fields are part of the Harry S. Truman Sports Complex.

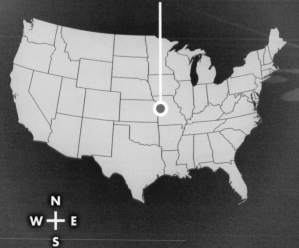

KANSAS CITY, MISSOURI

N
W E
S

CHIEFS

The Chiefs joined the National Football League (NFL) in 1970. They play in the American Football **Conference** (AFC). They are part of the West **Division**.

The West Division also includes the Denver Broncos, San Diego Chargers, and Oakland Raiders. Many fans consider the Chiefs' main **rivals** to be the Broncos and Raiders.

NFL DIVISIONS

AFC

AFC NORTH

BALTIMORE **RAVENS**

CINCINNATI **BENGALS**

CLEVELAND **BROWNS**

PITTSBURGH **STEELERS**

AFC EAST

BUFFALO **BILLS**

MIAMI **DOLPHINS**

NEW ENGLAND **PATRIOTS**

NEW YORK **JETS**

AFC SOUTH

HOUSTON **TEXANS**

INDIANAPOLIS **COLTS**

JACKSONVILLE **JAGUARS**

TENNESSEE **TITANS**

AFC WEST

DENVER **BRONCOS**

KANSAS CITY **CHIEFS**

OAKLAND **RAIDERS**

SAN DIEGO **CHARGERS**

NFC

NFC NORTH

 CHICAGO
BEARS

 DETROIT
LIONS

 GREEN BAY
PACKERS

 MINNESOTA
VIKINGS

NFC EAST

 DALLAS
COWBOYS

 NEW YORK
GIANTS

 PHILADELPHIA
EAGLES

 WASHINGTON
REDSKINS

NFC SOUTH

 ATLANTA
FALCONS

 CAROLINA
PANTHERS

 NEW ORLEANS
SAINTS

 TAMPA BAY
BUCCANEERS

NFC WEST

 ARIZONA
CARDINALS

 LOS ANGELES
RAMS

 SAN FRANCISCO
49ERS

SEATTLE
SEAHAWKS

In 1960, play in the AFL began. The Dallas Texans were among the original teams. They were one of the best teams in the AFL. But they were not the only team in Dallas. The city was also home to the NFL's Cowboys.

In 1963, the Texans moved to Kansas City. They were renamed the Chiefs.

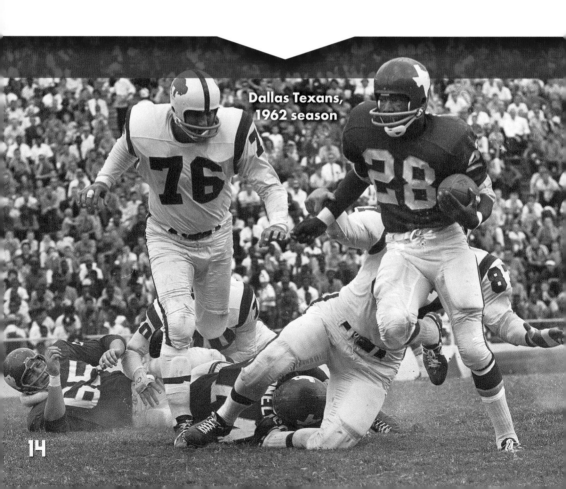

Dallas Texans, 1962 season

1963 season

15

In 1967, the Chiefs made it to the first-ever Super Bowl. They were the AFL team. The Green Bay Packers were the NFL team. The Packers won that championship. But a few years later, the Chiefs won Super Bowl 4.

SUPER BOWL 1
JANUARY 15, 1967

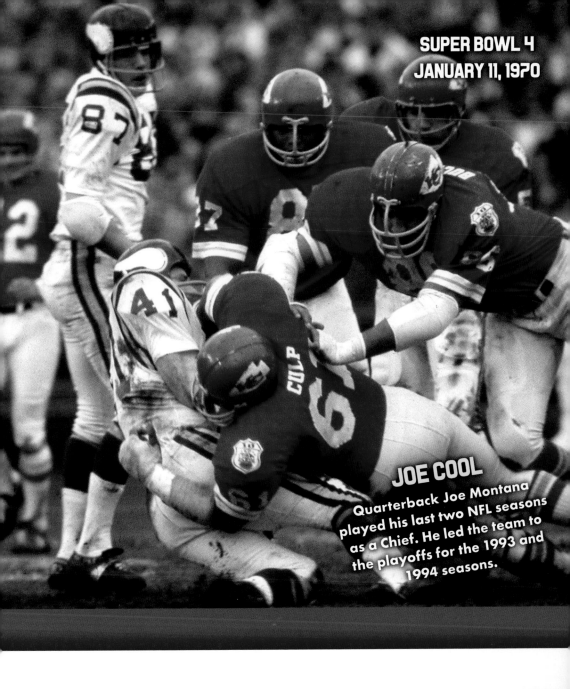

JOE COOL

Quarterback Joe Montana played his last two NFL seasons as a Chief. He led the team to the playoffs for the 1993 and 1994 seasons.

In the 1970s and 1980s, the Chiefs struggled in the NFL. But today, they are a solid playoff team.

TIMELINE

1960
Joined the AFL
(as the Dallas
Texans)

1963
Moved to Kansas
City, Missouri,
and changed their
name to the Chiefs

1967
Played in Super Bowl 1
after winning their second
AFL Championship, but lost
to the Green Bay Packers

10 FINAL SCORE **35**

1970
Joined
the NFL

1962
Won the AFL Championship,
beating the Houston Oilers
(20-17)

1970
Followed a third AFL
Championship with a
Super Bowl win, beating
the Minnesota Vikings

23 FINAL SCORE **7**

1989

Drafted Hall-of-Fame linebacker Derrick Thomas

2013

Hired head coach Andy Reid

1993

Traded for Hall-of-Fame quarterback Joe Montana

2008

Drafted running back Jamaal Charles

The Chiefs had stars on offense and defense for Super Bowl 4. Quarterback Len Dawson was named the game's Most Valuable Player (MVP). **Linebacker** and **defensive end** Bobby Bell helped on the defensive side.

Len Dawson

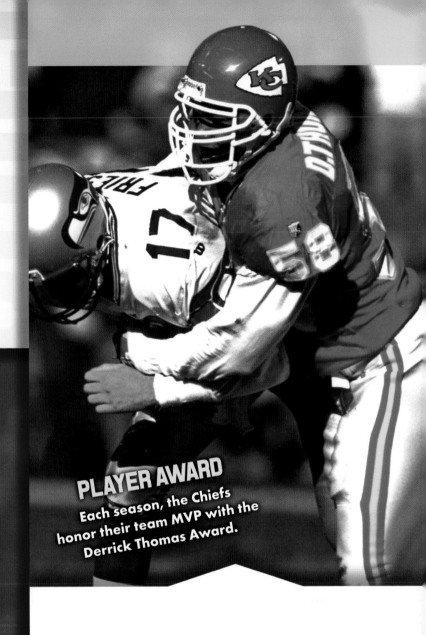

PLAYER AWARD
Each season, the Chiefs honor their team MVP with the Derrick Thomas Award.

In 1990, linebacker Derrick Thomas set an NFL record. In a game against the Seattle Seahawks, he had seven **sacks**!

The Chiefs have had some of the league's best tight ends. In 2008, Tony Gonzalez set a tight end record. It was for most career receiving yards. Today, Travis Kelce is a favorite target of quarterback Alex Smith.

Right now, most of the team's **rushing yards** come from running back Jamaal Charles. He is the Chiefs' all-time rushing leader.

TEAM GREATS

BOBBY BELL
LINEBACKER, DEFENSIVE END
1963-1974

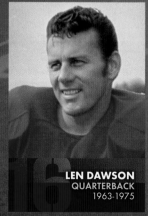

LEN DAWSON
QUARTERBACK
1963-1975

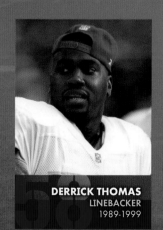

DERRICK THOMAS
LINEBACKER
1989-1999

Jamaal Charles

TOP RUNNING BACK

In 2001, running back Priest Holmes had 1,555 rushing yards to lead the league.

TONY GONZALEZ
TIGHT END
1997-2008

PRIEST HOLMES
RUNNING BACK
2001-2007

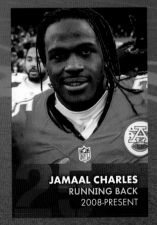

JAMAAL CHARLES
RUNNING BACK
2008-PRESENT

For many Chiefs fans, the excitement starts long before the game. No matter the weather, fans have pregame parties. They cook some Kansas City-style barbecue.

Before kickoff, Chiefs fans join in for the national anthem. Instead of finishing with "home of the brave," they proudly sing, "home of the Chiefs!"

Kansas City fans are passionate about their Chiefs. A sea of red and white fills Arrowhead Stadium for each game. They are proud and loud in support of their team.

Chiefs fans have held the Guinness record
for Loudest Stadium Cheers. They cheer their
team to victory!

MORE ABOUT THE
CHIEFS

Team name:
Kansas City Chiefs

Team name explained:
**Named for Kansas City
mayor H. Roe Bartle,
whose nickname was
"The Chief"**

**Joined NFL: 1970
(AFL from 1960-1969)**

Conference: AFC

Division: West

**Main rivals: Denver Broncos,
Oakland Raiders**

Hometown:
Kansas City, Missouri

Training camp location:
Missouri Western State University, St. Joseph, Missouri

KANSAS CITY

MISSOURI

N
W ✛ E
S

Home stadium name:
Arrowhead Stadium

Stadium opened: 1972

Seats in stadium: 76,416

Logo: An arrowhead with the letters KC, for Kansas City

Colors: Red, gold, white

Name for fan base: **Chiefs Kingdom**

Mascot: **KC Wolf**

GLOSSARY

conference—a large grouping of sports teams that often play one another

defense—the group of players who try to stop the opposing team from scoring

defensive end—a player on defense whose main job is to tackle the player with the ball

division—a small grouping of sports teams that often play one another; usually there are several divisions of teams in a conference.

linebacker—a player on defense whose main job is to make tackles and stop passes; a linebacker stands just behind the defensive linemen.

offense—the group of players who try to move down the field and score

playoffs—the games played after the regular NFL season is over; playoff games determine which teams play in the Super Bowl.

professional—a player or team that makes money playing a sport

quarterback—a player on offense whose main job is to throw and hand off the ball

rivals—teams that are long-standing opponents

running back—a player on offense whose main job is to run with the ball

rushing yards—yards gained by running with the ball

sacks—plays during which a player on defense tackles the opposing quarterback for a loss of yards

Super Bowl—the championship game for the NFL

tight end—a player on offense whose main jobs are to catch passes from the quarterback and to block defensive players

wide receiver—a player on offense whose main job is to catch passes from the quarterback

TO LEARN MORE

AT THE LIBRARY

Frisch, Nate. *The Story of the Kansas City Chiefs.* Mankato, Minn.: Creative Education, 2014.

Howell, Brian. *Kansas City Chiefs.* Mankato, Minn.: Child's World, 2015.

Wyner, Zach. *Kansas City Chiefs.* New York, N.Y.: AV2 by Weigl, 2015.

ON THE WEB

Learning more about the Kansas City Chiefs is as easy as 1, 2, 3.

1. Go to www.factsurfer.com.

2. Enter "Kansas City Chiefs" into the search box.

3. Click the "Surf" button and you will see a list of related web sites.

With factsurfer.com, finding more information is just a click away.

INDEX